Samuel French Acting Edition

Start Down

by Eleanor Burgess

SAMUELFRENCH.COM   SAMUELFRENCH.CO.UK

FOR PRODUCTION ENQUIRIES

UNITED STATES AND CANADA
Info@SamuelFrench.com
1-866-598-8449

UNITED KINGDOM AND EUROPE
Plays@SamuelFrench.co.uk
020-7255-4302

Each title is subject to availability from Samuel French, depending upon country of performance. Please be aware that *START DOWN* may not be licensed by Samuel French in your territory. Professional and amateur producers should contact the nearest Samuel French office or licensing partner to verify availability.

MUSIC USE NOTE

Licensees are solely responsible for obtaining formal written permission from copyright owners to use copyrighted music in the performance of this play and are strongly cautioned to do so. If no such permission is obtained by the licensee, then the licensee must use only original music that the licensee owns and controls. Licensees are solely responsible and liable for all music clearances and shall indemnify the copyright owners of the play(s) and their licensing agent, Samuel French, against any costs, expenses, losses and liabilities arising from the use of music by licensees. Please contact the appropriate music licensing authority in your territory for the rights to any incidental music.

IMPORTANT BILLING AND CREDIT REQUIREMENTS

If you have obtained performance rights to this title, please refer to your licensing agreement for important billing and credit requirements.

START DOWN was first produced by the Alliance Theatre (Susan Booth, Artistic Director; Jody Feldman, Producer) in Atlanta, Georgia on February 13, 2016. The production was directed by Jeremy Cohen, with sets and projections by Caite Hevner Kemp, costumes by Ivan Ingermann, lighting design by Josh Epstein, and sound design by Josh Horvath. The production stage manager was Rodney Williams. The cast was as follows:

WILL	Eric Sharp
SANDY	Annie Purcell
KAREN	Tracey Bonner
ADAM	Josh Tobin
MATTY	Andrew Puckett
JESSE	Anthony Campbell

CHARACTERS

(All ages are at the start of the play; the characters age three years.)

WILL – male, 28, Asian American, a programmer

SANDY – female, 28, secular Jewish, a history teacher

KAREN – female, 28, African American, a math teacher (also plays **E-KAREN**)

ADAM – male, 28, WASPy, a hedge fund analyst

MATTY – male, 23, a white Midwesterner, a programmer

JESSE – male, 16, African American, a high school student

XANDER – offstage voice*

*In past productions, the actor playing Matty has also been the voice of Xander.

SETTING

the Bay Area

TIME

the recent past to the near future

AUTHOR'S NOTES

You can do this play with set pieces for each location gliding on and offstage, or you can do it with only a few pieces of furniture, changing locations with props and light. You can do it with a lot of bells and whistles, or you can keep it very simple. Both versions work great.

The one crucial scenic element is the projections. The images should build in quality as the play goes on. A spectacular closing image will nail the meaning of the play for the audience.

You have permission to change the word "futon" in the script to suit the set choices you end up making.

Projection Note
A production license to perform *Start Down* does not include a license to publicly display any third-party or copyrighted images. Samuel French recommends licensees create their own images or use images in the public domain.

For Nick, for so many reasons

ACT ONE

Scene One

XANDER. *(Offstage.)* Ladies and gentlemen please take a moment to switch off your electronic vices. JK keep 'em on. Record this shit, it's gonna be awesome.

> *(Lights up on a sidewalk in SoMa. Sounds of a party several flights above.* **XANDER***'s mic'd voice booms from within.)*

Beloved friends, random fuckers – I'm Xander Montgomery, thank you so much for coming to celebrate with *Get Real Estate.*

So once upon a time, I was in college for like a hot minute.

> *(**WILL** enters, pulling on a jacket. He listens.)*

Like every college student in America, I wanted to buy booze. So, I hacked the student database and changed everyone's birthday so our student IDs would say we were twenty-one. That got me into the dean's office.

And he said to me – "You're too clever for your own good."

And I realized – that place had nothing to teach me.

We are clever for everybody's good.

> *(Cheers from the party. Each word is a small stab for* **WILL***, but he can't stop listening.)*

Most people, they spend their lives *accepting.* TV networks say if you wanna watch our show you gotta be home Tuesday at eight, and people say – "Okay." Real estate brokers say you can't look for your own apartment and people say – "Okay."

(**SANDY** *enters from the party. Reads* **WILL***'s mood.*)

XANDER. *(Offstage.)* We are the people who wonder – isn't there a better way to do this? And we don't just *wonder* if there's a better way – we build it. We make a better way available for everybody else.

WILL. Two point five x surge pricing, seven minute wait.

XANDER. *(Offstage.) We make shit people love.* So drink up me hearties. And keep being clever, for everybody's good!

(*Cheers. Music comes on.* * *Something aggressive and obnoxious.*)

SANDY. I will say – 200 million dollar acquisition, he could have sprung for nicer finger food.

WILL. It was a 248 million dollar acquisition.

SANDY. And I don't know why he opened the speech "ladies and gentlemen." I'm pretty sure I was one of four ladies there.

And I did not see a single gentleman.

I did see some bros. Browskis. Bromobiles.

"For everybody's good." I'm sorry like listing luxury apartments online is *saving America*?

WILL. He's amped up.

SANDY. Why aren't you joining me in making fun of the brogrammers?

WILL. Because I would like to be brogramming as successfully as they are.

SANDY. You don't want to be them. They're obnoxious.

WILL. Then I would like to be as obnoxious as they are because it is *really* working for them.

(*Beat.*)

---

*A license to produce *Start Down* does not include a performance license for any third-party or copyrighted music. Licensees should create an original composition or use music in the public domain. For further information, please see Music Use Note on page 3.

SANDY. ...Did your father call?

WILL. He just wanted to tell me that Berkeley would probably still take me back.

And that he did not give up his entire life and move across an ocean so that I could be a quitter.

SANDY. He's not used to the modern economy. He probably thinks if you'd finished your PhD you'd have tenure by now, but the people who do big important stuff now don't follow that straight of a path.

WILL. I am working for a company that's making *Facebook for pets*.

SANDY. There was a strategy behind joining The Social Petwork! You said you'd get a job at a company you wouldn't feel bound to, you'd pay off your loans, you'd learn the ropes –

WILL. I'm twenty-eight.

SANDY. Yeah that's fine for men that's like twelve.

WILL. For startups it's like sixty-four.

SANDY. In 1850 a twenty-*nine*-year-old captain in the U.S. Army was forced to resign because of rumored drunkenness. So he took over part of his brother-in-law's farm in Missouri where he proceeded to lose money for four years. And his name was Ulysses S. Grant.

WILL. You're saying I should hope for civil war.

SANDY. I'm saying your opportunity will come. You will find an idea – an *important* one – and you'll do something amazing. Because you are smarter and better than those brobots.

You don't actually want to be Xander, do you?

WILL. No. You're right. His company's so stupid. That's what makes it so horrible – he's not doing anything significant or helpful or life-changing but everyone's *idolizing* him. I just want to matter.

(**SANDY** *puts her arms around him.*)

SANDY. You matter to me.

(Beat. No answer from **WILL.***)*

SANDY. Maybe you should try to get dinner with Xander sometime. Get his advice.

WILL. Eugh. I hate asking for favors from a –
No that's smart though.
Hey he doesn't have to work anymore maybe he's free tomorrow.

SANDY. Tomorrow's dinner with Karen and Adam.

WILL. Oh fuck.

SANDY. What it'll be fun.

WILL. No. It will be them listing nice things they've done in the last month. Like, "Oh, the powder at Squaw was *so* much deeper than Vail. And we ate at this divine little place that had subarctic char sashimi –"

SANDY. That is not a thing.

WILL. I cannot stand it when people list things they've eaten. I cannot stand it. It is not an accomplishment to eat things.

SANDY. I asked if you were up for it this month and you agreed. It's on your calendar.

*(***WILL*** checks. It's there. This annoys him.)*

WILL. It is very frustrating to me that you are always right.

Scene Two

(The next night. A dinner party is in progress at Karen and Adam's apartment in Pacific Heights. They're phasing out of IKEA.)

KAREN. He "wanted to see a wet t-shirt contest."

ADAM. Well he is a fourteen-year-old boy.

KAREN. He's also an idiot. The sprinklers only go off if there's smoke. If you pull a lever all that happens is a loud unpleasant noise and a waste of time.

SANDY. *And* you get purple ink on your hand, and they find you and you miss *two weeks of class* –

KAREN. I hate the suspension policy.

SANDY. All sane people should hate the suspension policy. "Hey kids, do something wrong and get two weeks off"? If a student is misbehaving obviously the best way to punish him is *more class* –

KAREN. After-school help. Research projects.

SANDY. But no, Frankie Hayes is going to miss two weeks of school, and then he'll be behind –

KAREN. – He'll feel alienated in class –

SANDY. – And he'll drop out early and his life will suck!

ADAM. All because he wanted to see a wet t-shirt contest. There's something very deep and eternal about that.

KAREN. So I was about to offer dessert before Sandy and I abducted the conversation. Anyone interested in roasted cacao or salted caramel truffles from CocoaBella? And Adam picked out a wonderful Sauternes to go with them.

WILL. *Great.*

SANDY. That sounds awesome.

*(**KAREN** begins clearing dishes.)*

No Karen do not do that, you cooked all of this! I cleared the appetizers, and I got here early to help arrange cheese and I am now looking for one of the men to maybe pitch the fuck in. No offense.

(**ADAM** *and* **WILL** *start clearing plates.*)

ADAM. It's so great to have you two over. Very few people order me around in my own home. Besides her, obviously.

KAREN. *I do not.*

(**ADAM** *and* **WILL** *go.*)

SANDY. God this place is spectacular. I think the last time I saw it –

KAREN. We didn't have the new furniture yet.

SANDY. And the view! I think it was foggy the last time I was here. You can see the bridge!
That is ridiculous.
Are you worried about the rent going up?

KAREN. We might try to buy actually, when the lease is up.

SANDY. Oh wow.

KAREN. Yeah, look for somewhere with a little more space. Maybe a couple more bedrooms...

SANDY. Ahh, don't even say it! Is that what's happening, is that the life stage we're in now?

KAREN. It's just practical to look now. Everyone says after the next few IPOs the prices'll be impossible.

(**ADAM** *and* **WILL** *re-enter with dessert.*)

WILL. It's not the graphics it's the gameplay. You have constant choices, do you want to stage an attack? Or go into stealth mode –

ADAM. Will has the new Call of Duty!

KAREN. Boys and their toys.

SANDY. Karen and Adam are buying a house.

KAREN. An *apartment.*

SANDY. Karen and Adam are buying a three-bedroom apartment.

KAREN. It's – Adam's parents have been really generous. They want to give it as a wedding present.

WILL. Wow. That's nice.

ADAM. Yeah I mean it's not really my parents. They're – it's a loan – but I think we would have anyways. It's just a sound investment. You know in the end you *save* money buying.

WILL. Right. Of course.

ADAM. *(Opening the wine.)* Fun fact – did you know sweet wines are sweet because the grapes get attacked by a fungus? The fungus eats five-sixths of the acid in the wine but only one-third of the sugar. It's called "the noble rot."

WILL. So how else was the faculty meeting? Before you got evacuated.

KAREN. Typical September stuff. They announce new initiatives every year. As if announcing was accomplishing. Like, you know what's been wrong with struggling schools all these years? It's that they never thought to *announce* that they wanted good test scores!

ADAM. What are the initiatives du jour?

KAREN. Oh god, can I even remember all of them.

SANDY. I made an acronym. TITDOME.

KAREN. Okay – Technology. Innovation. T... The Transparency initiative, which is supposed to help parents understand grading? With god knows how much paperwork.

SANDY. I know you know the next one.

KAREN. *Diversification.* Ooo boy.

WILL. Um. Isn't the school already...diverse?

SANDY. It's diverse lesson plans. You know how the classes are – you have kids who are gifted in a subject and kids who've scraped by with a D for five years and they just can't do the same work.

KAREN. When I teach trigonometry, some of the kids in the class still need practice with fractions or decimals. Now they're saying I'm supposed to have a different lesson plan for each student. Different worksheets, different exercises.

WILL. That sounds like a good thing.

KAREN. What's that?

WILL. If a student can't do fractions it seems stupid to give them trig problems.

KAREN. Sure, ideally it wouldn't happen. But I have thirty-five to forty students each in six classes. How exactly does the superintendent expect me to make 230 worksheets a day?

SANDY. Adderall.

WILL. It seems like software could do a much better job handling that work.

ADAM. Like the GREs! You take the GREs on a computer, if you get a question wrong it sends you easier questions, if you get a bunch right it sends you harder questions.

SANDY. When did you take the GREs?

ADAM. You are forgetting that year when I wanted to be a psychologist.

KAREN. It's not a question of "easy" or "hard." When I'm grading, there are particular skills I'm looking for. It takes training to recognize where a kid's going wrong.

SANDY. I can't believe grading is starting again.

ADAM. Need more wine?

WILL. Another advantage of software would be that it could grade. The second a kid finishes a question it could tell you if they got it right.

ADAM. Wow. Imagine that Kare. No grading to take home.

SANDY. Oh man, invent that for history.
(Robot voice.) Thesis does not compute.

WILL. And the feedback would be immediate. I mean when I was in school, by the time the teachers got anything back to us we forgot the test had ever happened. It was a joke.

KAREN. A joke?

WILL. Yeah, every day, you'd say do you have my test, and they'd have some lame excuse like – oh, no my dog got herpes and I was too busy –

KAREN. – Living a complicated adult life, to wait on your every adolescent need?

WILL. No it's really hard, I get it. That's my point.

What if it could be easier?

KAREN. There *is* a way to make this job easier. And that is to hire more teachers and have normal-sized classrooms.

ADAM. At my high school classes were capped at fourteen.

WILL. That's definitely one way. But it's really expensive. Teachers have pensions, medical bills.

SANDY. How dare they.

KAREN. Kids today don't need to spend more time staring at screens. What they need is more personal attention from people who can understand and guide them.

WILL. No – totally – totally. That makes sense.

But if they can't get that –

KAREN. Look, you don't know what you're talking about.

WILL. I'm going off what you told me. And based on that it seems like maybe –

KAREN. I'm not good enough at my job?

WILL. I don't mean that. Don't get offended.

KAREN. Don't be offensive.

ADAM. ...Hey Will, let's be manly men and go clean the kitchen.

> (**WILL, SANDY,** *and* **ADAM** *carry dishes offstage.*
> **KAREN** *toes off her heels. Lights change – it's*
> *later.* **ADAM** *re-enters with a last glass of wine.*)

KAREN. He's like a human troll. I don't know how she puts up with it.

ADAM. With what?

KAREN. With him picking at everything, questioning everything. Instead of having a little respect. It's exhausting.

ADAM. I think in his field it's really valuable. In college everyone wanted to do problem sets with him, he wouldn't let you be lazy.

KAREN. Remember that time he brought up affirmative action? Who does that? Who thinks, "There are members of three races here, someone should bring up affirmative action."

ADAM. Will. Will does that.

KAREN. Do you think he has Asperger's?

ADAM. No I think he just really doesn't mind offending people.

KAREN. That was bad. I did not mean to make a joke about a disability, that was not funny.

ADAM. Yeah. You're a terrible person.

KAREN. I never thought there was such a thing as having too many critical thinking skills but he has taught me to see the world in a whole new way.

ADAM. What do you want to do with the last night of summer Ms. Green?

KAREN. Check my materials. Check my work bag. Do my bedtime ritual and get my seven hours.

ADAM. Not the answer I had in mind.

KAREN. Well, at least you know I'll always be honest with you.

ADAM. The same can be said of Will.

KAREN. Oh god.

(She laughs and exits. **ADAM** *follows.)*

(Will and Sandy's apartment. They're still in the IKEA phase. **WILL** *enters, pacing.)*

WILL. I hate it when people think that having feelings means they don't have to deal with logic.

Like hey, instead of responding to the intelligent and well-thought-out point you just made,

I'll just say I'm hurt by your ideas, and you won't be allowed to keep talking, which means,

I'll never need to acknowledge that you're actually right.

*(***SANDY*** *enters in boxers and a ratty t-shirt.)*

SANDY. I found a new mole.

*(She holds out her arm. **WILL** takes a look.)*

WILL. I like your moles.

SANDY. I like that your hair's so thick. I don't think you're gonna go bald.

> *(**WILL** puts his toes over her toes. This is a little game. **SANDY** tries to pull her toes away and put them over his toes. It leads to a small toe war in which she almost falls over. She laughs.)*

WILL. Hey can I ask you a question?

SANDY. Of course.

WILL. What did you think of the program idea?

SANDY. Um. I think it maybe wasn't the most sensitive possible conversation topic.

WILL. I mean as like an *idea* idea.

For a company.

SANDY. Oh. Wow. Wow. Um.

So the idea is – software. With math problems. That adjusts the difficulty based on how a student is doing.

WILL. And grades. Sends the teacher a report, that kind of thing.

SANDY. It sounds maybe useful.

...I do agree with Karen that kids don't need more time with screens.

WILL. For sure. I just think – hiring more teachers? That's not gonna happen. Like good for you if you're Adam and your grandfather like invented shipping containers and you can pay for tiny classrooms, but say you're the smart kid in a public school classroom –

SANDY. Hard to imagine, but I'll try.

WILL. You shouldn't have to be bored, you should be challenged.

SANDY. ...I'll tell you what. Schools would love it.

WILL. Yeah?

SANDY. Definitely.

Education's like parenting. No one knows what the heck they're doing.

There are a million theories about how to do it, and they all contradict each other. But if we could *track* how students were doing day by day... If we had data on what they were getting and what they weren't... What results they got with different textbooks or different styles of teaching... Maybe we could figure a couple things out.

(She exits.)

WILL. How many public school students are there in America?

SANDY. *(Offstage.)* Forty-eight million. Give or take.

WILL. *(That's an enormous market.)* Wow.

(**SANDY** *re-enters, applying face cream.*)

SANDY. You know what I'd do if I were a math teacher? Let's say two-thirds of the class is getting something. I'd put them on the software and I'd work with the ones who were behind.

WILL. You'd make a small class within a big class.

SANDY. Exactly. You could do the same for the advanced kids. Have most of the class get some basic practice while you teach a few kids a special enrichment lesson. Math games, independent study.

WILL. They'd get *more* personal attention.

And the thing is – Math is one of the most meritocratic fields. If you're a poor kid, if you can just learn enough math to get an engineering degree, you have a future.

SANDY. And then – what if they all went out into the world ready to become primary care physicians? And environmental engineers. And better teachers and non-stupid congresspeople –

WILL. Okay you are very utopian –

(**SANDY** *jumps up on the futon.*)

SANDY. No – no cynicism! What if we actually used all of the potential of every kid coming out of every classroom in America. And they could *vote* smarter, which means America gets better which means the world gets better, and we don't die in nuclear war and we colonize Saturn and spread art and hope and philosophy to the far corners of the universe!

WILL. Why are you on the futon?

SANDY. We don't keep a soapbox around.

> (**WILL** *puts his arms around her and tries to pull her down. She tries to stay put – a little tug of war.*)

WILL. Get off your soapbox!

SANDY. Never!

WILL. Get off your soapbox!

> (**SANDY** *shrieks as he swoops her down off the couch. He kisses her. The kiss becomes serious.*)

> (*Still kissing her, he walks her toward the bedroom. Her foot bumps the couch.*)

SANDY. Ow!

> (*Still kissing, they tug each other offstage.*)

> (*The sounds of a high school hallway. Shrieks. Yelling. Clanging lockers. Chaos. A school bell rings.*)

> (**SANDY** *enters in a long skirt and a ruffled blouse. She looks like someone from the early nineteenth century – a Gibson Girl. She steps forward in front of the apartments to address the audience.*)

Hey class! Welcome to Twentieth Century History. *(Of her outfit.)* I thought that I would do something to bring the history alive for you. In retrospect that may have been a dorky decision.

History classes usually begin with a first class on why we should study history.

Most teachers will tell you something about how you can only know what *will* happen if you know what *has* happened.

I think that's stupid. No one knows what will happen.

My plug is that studying history is the best way to develop empathy.

When you're studying history, the key thing is to remember that it all happened to *people*.

Real people, just like you, whose necks got itchy, used to wear clothing like this every day.

Life would have smelled worse. Why? How did people get around?

Yes, horses! There would be horse poop *everywhere*. How about refrigerators? Nope!

Just iceboxes. Literally boxes with ice in them. Imagine the mold. But then the food would have been fresh. The idea of food coming out of a box was not a thing.

This classroom would have been impossible. What might I mean by that?

Schools in California *were* segregated, but in an unusual way. Hispanic students were forced to go to Spanish-language schools. That wouldn't change until Méndez v. Westminster. In *1946*. And boys usually dropped out of school by sixth grade to work.

Imagine.

When you study history you have to imagine what it feels like to be a totally different human being, from a totally different life. And being able to imagine that is the key to being a good person.

Okay. Get out your books and turn to page one.

Scene Three

*(Three weeks later. The Social Petwork offices –
part of a coworking space in SoMa.)*

*(**MATTY** and **WILL** may throw a mini basketball
back and forth as they talk. Maybe there's
even a mini basketball hoop. If so, **MATTY**
always misses.)*

MATTY. Who else is on board?

WILL. Nobody.

MATTY. Are you freaking kidding? You've never started a
company.

WILL. No one else has ever started a company until they
start a company.

MATTY. Yeah and lots of people try to start a company and
fail.

WILL. You know for a twenty-three-year-old you are really
chicken shit.

MATTY. For a twenty-three-year-old, I make 95,000 a year,
I show up for work sometime between noon and 2:30
and I still get off work in time to meet a beautiful lady
and go back to her place.

WILL. That is not true.

MATTY. Well I have time to meet them anyway.

WILL. What are you working on this week?

(No answer.)

What are you working on this week?

MATTY. Making the birthday calendar convertible to dog
years.

WILL. Making the birthday calendar convertible to dog
years. Matty. You're the fastest coder I know and you're
busy adding a moronic feature to a fourth-rate site.
I built a prototype.

*(The actress playing **KAREN** appears – but it's
not Karen. She looks different – washed in
projections, or bathed in blue light.)*

E-KAREN.	MATTY.
If one side of a triangle is forty-eight inches, and the hypotenuse is seventy-three inches, the remaining side is A: fifty-five, B: 311, C: eighteen.	Ew you're gonna let it use inches?

MATTY. The program's generating each problem on its own?

WILL. I taught it the Pythagorean theorem. For now the wrong answers are random integers.

MATTY. Not bad.

WILL. The *trick* is – if it could not just be right or wrong, but if it could catch what a student isn't getting.

E-KAREN. If one side of a triangle is twenty-five decimeters and the hypotenuse is twenty-nine decimeters, the remaining side is A: twenty-nine. Missing the unit of measurement! B: thirty-eight decimeters. Wrong side!

MATTY. So the program needs a formula for human error??

WILL. I said it would be difficult. That's why I want your help.

MATTY. Plus those problems are crazy repetitive. Say you're the smart kid, how do they get harder?

WILL. Larger numbers?

E-KAREN. If the hypotenuse is 286,000 miles –

MATTY. No, just no.

WILL. So you mean you want. What...word problems?

MATTY. Ew.

WILL. I hated word problems.

MATTY. I know. They're all like, let's say there's a lamppost. You improbably happen to know that the lamppost's twelve feet tall, and that its shadow is six feet tall, and you for no conceivable fucking reason *really* want to figure out –

WILL. They're bullshit.

(Beat.)

MATTY. You know what I would like to see is a word problem that's like – so King Kong has gone on a rampage through New York, and he's knocked over the Empire State Building, which is 400 meters high and forty meters wide, and the average density of people in New York is a hundred per hundred square meters, how many people just died?

WILL. Wait. What if that was like – our thing?

MATTY. King Kong word problems? Calm down man, it's not actually like *that* good of an idea.

WILL. No I mean – what if we could come up with really really awesome problems that kids would *want* to solve –

MATTY. Like – when should you do a wall shot versus a direct shot in pool?

WILL. Can a person duck fast enough to avoid a bullet?

E-KAREN. If Mick Jagger has slept with eight women a week for the last forty years, how many times has he had gonorrhea?

WILL. What if – what if we hired really smart creative like young not emotionally dead people to write our word problems? So that if the kids proved they could handle the simple problems, the questions got harder and harder and cooler and cooler...

MATTY. It's a big expense. Hiring all those people.

WILL. But it's a one-time expense. The kids move on, next year's kids can use the same problems. And it's scalable – you could sell the exact same set of problems to more and more schools –

MATTY. And if we're hiring people to do the problems – if they're not algorithmic...

Will we don't have to stick to math.

You could have people write multiple-choice questions about...To Kill a Fucking Mockingbird.

WILL. Software for use by every student, every day, in every subject.

MATTY. *Fuck yeah.*

> (**MATTY** *and* **WILL** *exit.*)
>
> (*A bar in Oakland.* **KAREN** *and* **SANDY** *enter with margaritas.*)

SANDY. I can't freaking believe it –

KAREN. After four years how are you still surprised?

SANDY. I'm sorry like there's *no* money to keep the mentoring program going. There's *no* money to pay for classroom decorations –

KAREN. Or college counseling.

SANDY. – Or photocopying more than *two sheets per student per day*, but it's still possible to hire a *third* assistant principle –

KAREN. Sandy you're yelling at the choir.

SANDY. I think all administrators should be required to still be classroom teachers for at least one class a year.

KAREN. Are we playing imaginary school again?

SANDY. Maybe. Do you prefer Sandy Prep or Sandy Academy?

KAREN. So I wanted to get a drink with you because –

SANDY. Because it's Friday and on Fridays we drink?

KAREN. Because I wanted to ask if you'd be one of my bridesmaids.

SANDY. Oh my god. Really? That's – wow. I mean yay! Oh – I'm honored.

KAREN. Really? I mean I know it's a lot –
I just wanted to – if it's weird at all, you know that's totally –

SANDY. No – No! Why would it be weird?

KAREN. Just – I know you and Will have been dating longer. I mean you guys introduced us.

SANDY. No! No. Are you kidding? That is totally – that's *fine*.

KAREN. Good, good – I just wanted to check.

SANDY. It's *totally* fine.

KAREN. I mean of course, you guys are great. I'm so old-fashioned. I told Adam right from the beginning we both had two years to make up our minds.

SANDY. Seriously?

KAREN. Yeah.

(**SANDY** *snorts.*)

What?

SANDY. You like your deadlines.

(*Beat.*)

KAREN. Do you ever wonder whether it's a bad sign that you and Will haven't taken that step?

SANDY. No. Will and I are great.

KAREN. Of course. But Will can be – a difficult person.

SANDY. He's a challenging person. But I like being challenged. He's literally my best friend.

KAREN. Sorry I'm – I'm thinking of what I'd want.

I'm so so glad you'll be there with me on the big day.

SANDY. Damn right I will.

No, I will tell you what would not be okay – if you choose taffeta bridesmaids dresses – in that case I'm out –

(**KAREN**'s *laughing as her cell phone rings.*)

KAREN. Oh god.

SANDY. You don't have to get it now!

KAREN. I made a deal with those kids, call me anytime and I *will* pick up. Okay, let's see how well I explain logarithms after a margarita.

(*Into her phone, as she exits.*) Hi Maria.

SANDY. I'm getting you a second one!!

(*She exits, headed to the bar.*)

(*Karen and Adam's apartment.* **WILL** *sits, attempting to be at ease.*)

ADAM. (*Offstage.*) Will, you want wine or beer? Or bourbon, I have a great new bourbon.

WILL. Um, beer. Beer.

ADAM. *(Offstage.)* You want a lager, or more of an IPA?

WILL. Just beer, man.

ADAM. *(Offstage.)* Haha, fair enough.

> *(He enters, hands* **WILL** *a beer.* **WILL** *points to a new silver bowl on the table.)*

WILL. That's a cool – thing.

ADAM. Engagement present.

WILL. Sweet.

ADAM. Yeah it's a little annoying – you're supposed to ask for household objects, and really what I want is something more like Warriors tickets? But yeah. It feels classy.

WILL. Definitely.

ADAM. You said you wanted some advice?

WILL. Yeah... In a couple of months, we're going to be looking for seed investors. And I was wondering whether you had any advice. For pitching. I figure you evaluate companies all the time at the fund.

ADAM. Yeah, we do. Um. Is this for the social petbook thing? I thought you were quitting –

WILL. Yeah, I did! I'm doing my own thing.

ADAM. Good for you, man.

WILL. I'm actually looking at – you remember that thing I talked about with Karen?

ADAM. You mean the thing you *argued* about with Karen? Dude oh my god. Don't tell her I'm talking about this with you. You'll get me in trouble.

WILL. Sure. Sure. But I did some research. It's something there's really a need for.

> *(He hands* **ADAM** *a printout.)*

ADAM. Interesting.

WILL. There are samples of the style of questions on the next page.

> *(**ADAM** reads. He chuckles at one or two.)*

ADAM. I guess, if I were evaluating this as a pitch – I'd have questions about the risks. It's a high upfront cost. And a tough product to refine.

WILL. But I can do it.

ADAM. Well, yeah, *I* know you can. But VCs won't know you personally.

WILL. So you think I can do it.

ADAM. Sure. You're super smart and totally pigheaded, those seem like the right traits for a CEO. But there are safer investments out there.

WILL. There are safer investments if all you want is a good return. At a hedge fund I get it. You have investors depending on you, rich people need a place to keep their cash...

WILL.	**ADAM**.
I just think for Silicon Valley guys – they also want to know they're helping change the world.	Well, that's not –

ADAM. Well. All investing changes the world. It makes things possible.

WILL. I mean...betting on a horse race isn't riding a horse.

ADAM. Well I wouldn't lead with that.

WILL. Of course not. I just meant – *Classrooms are broken.* Imagine if you went into a hospital with appendicitis and the doctor pulled out a bottle of ether and a hacksaw. There is no other industry where it's still considered okay to do things the way they were done in the nineteenth century. But in schools...

ADAM. It's still one grownup, standing at the front of the class, talking to a bunch of kids. Like it's the Middle Ages.

WILL. I want to change that. I want to be able to say that was me, I changed that.

ADAM. That doesn't mean jumping on every potential idea –

WILL. But this is a growth field. EdTech is the new frontier. I think in a couple years, everyone is going to be going into it. Not doing it now will be like – saying no to Facebook when it first started. You'd want to shoot yourself. You'd never get over the fact that you didn't do it.

ADAM. What does Sandy think?

WILL. She loves the idea. That's the best part.

Students learn more, teachers have more time, we make money. Everybody wins.

ADAM. Maybe.

WILL. Think about it – education. It fixes everything.

Think about kids across America being smarter because of you. And the economy running better because of you, and voters voting more intelligently because of you.

Like your grandfather, right?

Every time you see Made in Taiwan stuck on something, that was him. He changed everything. I'm going to change everything. And all I need is a little bit of money.

ADAM. Wait a second – are you asking for advice or are you pitching me?

WILL. Either one that gets me money.

ADAM. You're a sonofabitch Will.

WILL. Maybe I just thought you were a man of good taste.

ADAM. How much exactly do you think you need?

Scene Four

*(Six weeks later. Sandy's classroom. There's a whiteboard. **SANDY** sits behind a teacher's desk. **JESSE** sits opposite her, a backpack at his feet. He's fidgety, uncomfortable. He shifts his weight, jiggles his leg...)*

JESSE. I only missed like a couple minutes.

SANDY. That isn't the problem. The problem is that I'm seeing a pattern.

I think this is maybe the fifth or sixth time you've fallen asleep in class.

JESSE. Okay.

SANDY. Okay?

JESSE. It's okay with me.

SANDY. Is there something going on?

Is there a reason you're not getting enough sleep? / Homework stuff?

JESSE. No. I get it done.

SANDY. Is there something going on at home?

JESSE. No.

SANDY. You can talk to me.

JESSE. There's literally nothing going on at home.

I'm passing.

SANDY. I know that.

JESSE. So, I don't know why I'm here.

I mean there are other kids talking during class like, Kyle plays games on his phone literally every day, I don't see why I'm here and he's not here.

SANDY. Do you know how it affects class when you fall asleep?

Probably not, because you're asleep so you can't see it, but you can imagine.

They're giggling, they're waiting for me to react.

And learning gets a little harder for everybody.

JESSE. I get it.

SANDY. You do?

JESSE. Yeah.

SANDY. It affects everybody else in the room. Do you understand that?

You understand that you're affecting other people?

JESSE. Well maybe if you don't want me to fall asleep class should be less boring.

SANDY. Excuse me?

JESSE. I'm just saying.

SANDY. ...What exactly are you "just saying"?

JESSE. I'm saying if I'm falling asleep isn't that kind of your fault.

SANDY. Well, thirty-four students *aren't* falling asleep, so...

You know a lot of kids *love* my classes. I have students come back and take electives from me their senior year, they tell their siblings to try to have me –

JESSE. Okay.

SANDY. But if you won't put any *effort* in –

JESSE. Okay. Never mind.

SANDY. You know Charles Bukowski said, "Only the boring get bored."

JESSE. Okay. I'm boring.

SANDY. No. No, I'm sorry.

That was not – right. That was not right. I'm a little tired.

I would really like to hear what you have to say about class.

JESSE. Whatever. It's fine.

SANDY. Look, um.

Can you – tell me something about yourself? What's a thing you like?

JESSE. I don't know. Food. Normal stuff.

SANDY. Tell me something about you that I wouldn't know.

JESSE. I'm allergic to tree nuts.

SANDY. Tell me something you're proud of.

JESSE. Um.

I have a YouTube channel. I do like, product reviews. TV episode reviews. Talk about stuff that's cool. Or messed up. Stuff like that.

SANDY. Jesse! That's *so cool*. That's really neat!

JESSE. *Neat?*

SANDY. Do I sound fifty? I do, don't I? I'll have you know that I have watched the YouTubes. I think that's really cool.

JESSE. Thanks.

SANDY. Honestly Jesse I should not say this but until today, I would have thought you were a boring person. Whatever energy you have, whatever personality you bring to those videos...you bring *none* of that to class.

JESSE. Well. It's *class*.

SANDY. Look, what's one thing I could do to teach you better?

I'm totally serious. What's one thing I could do?

JESSE. Let us out earlier.

SANDY. You know I can't do that.

JESSE. Don't assign homework. I don't know.

SANDY. Take your time.

> *(He does. He's uncomfortable with an adult suddenly taking him this seriously.)*

JESSE. You talk kind of fast sometimes. It's easy to fall behind.

And – you could write more neatly on the board. Like, be more clear about, do we have to know stuff. Cuz sometimes you say, "You don't have to know this, this is just interesting," but then suddenly you're back to stuff we *do* have to know, and it's confusing.

SANDY. Okay. I hear that.

JESSE. And don't give us a hard time about bathroom breaks.

SANDY. I don't give you a hard time –

JESSE. Like, "Oh, not right now," and then, "Five more minutes," and then class is over.

SANDY. Ha, right, fair enough.

JESSE. And don't call on Shoshanna all the time –

SANDY. Okay! Okay. I promise to work on that.

If I do...will you speak up once per class?

JESSE. Speak up how?

SANDY. Any way. Ask a question. Offer information.

Talk about stuff that's cool, or messed up. In history, obviously.

I think you should try to figure out what *you* have to add.

What's no one going to say if you don't say it?

Can you do that?

JESSE. Yeah.

SANDY. Awesome. *Neat.*

JESSE. Can I go now? I have work.

SANDY. Sure. Sure. Of course.

> (**JESSE** *gets up and heads for the door.*)

JESSE. Um. Alejandra's outside. In the hall.

SANDY. Great. Send her in.

> (**JESSE** *leaves.* **SANDY** *guzzles from a cup of coffee. She tries to reset.*)
>
> (**MATTY** *and* **WILL** *enter.* **MATTY** *eats potato chips.* **WILL** *takes notes on the whiteboard.*)

WILL. Can you remember a time when you really loved school?

> (**SANDY** *exits.*)

MATTY. Ummm. Snow days.

The time school was cancelled because of a tornado.

The time school was cancelled because of a bomb threat.

WILL. Don't be stupid come on.

MATTY. Field trips? Okay okay don't get fussy –

...I had a teacher for Western Civ. Who had us do a debate. Who mattered more, Luther or Napoleon? I liked that.

WILL. You mean like – the speaking part of it?

MATTY. I think I just liked winning?

WILL. Yeah. So if we can make it competitive. A challenge.

(**E-KAREN** *appears.*)

E-KAREN. Cassie spotted fifteen errors in this paragraph. Can you find more?

MATTY. Would it make people nervous? If they're afraid they're gonna look stupid –

WILL. They can have a choice. Everyone gets to have a choice.

E-KAREN. Wanna keep going on your own, or challenge Jared to a race? Okay! On your marks, get set...

(**SANDY** *enters, dressed as Rosie the Riveter. She spins the whiteboard around and starts a neatly-written list of "important terms.")*

SANDY. Shawn you have fifteen seconds to make it to your seat and open your notebook before –

(The bell rings.)

Good morning awesome kids! Okay. On the sixteenth of July, 1945, Harry Truman got a very important telegram from New Mexico. Manuela, what did it say? Nope, that is a good guess, but do I like it when we guess?

No! I like it when we use our brains and figure things out.

Cory, did you become Manuela at some point?

Okay then it's not your turn. What's going on in New Mexico?

Yes. Good. Thousands of nerds have been hanging out in New Mexico for three years, and on the sixteenth of July, 1945 Truman gets a telegram. It worked. Yes, boom!

Truman now has the world's most powerful and lethal weapon. Mel Gibson! Just kidding. The atomic bomb. And Truman has a choice – should he use it?

Okay everyone do a turn and talk, come up with three reasons, yes or no, meanwhile I'm gonna come around and check your homework so have that out too.

> *(She adds "atomic bomb," "Harry Truman," and "Manhattan Project" to her terms list.)*

WILL. Do you remember anything you learned? I'm going over these state tests and there's stuff in here that I know I learned, because I freaking aced those tests, but now I have no idea.

MATTY. Hit me.

WILL. Ionic bonds.

MATTY. Those are a thing. In which...molecules? Exchange ions.

WILL. Past perfect progressive tense.

> **(MATTY** *makes a "fucked if I know" face.)*

The Treaty of Guadalupe Hidalgo.

MATTY. That's the thing man, of course I don't remember. School doesn't work.

WILL. ...Name every Red Hot Chili Peppers album in order.

MATTY. That's different. I was into them.

WILL. So let's let people work on stuff they're into.

E-KAREN. Want to practice footnoting with an article on football, otters or Beyoncé?

> *(Slivers of light appear, flickering on the desks, whiteboard, wall. They lap at the scene's edges.)*

SANDY. So, Christian, you're Truman's advisor – what do you think he should do?

Um, drop it. You can't just tell the president, "Um, drop it." I think you can do better.

Okay, Christian says drop it instead of invading in order to *save troop lives.*

That's a great question. I don't know how many people had died so far in the Pacific. A lot. Crystal, you have my permission to look it up on your phone, and then to put that phone back in your backpack.

(She writes down what Crystal says: "Okinawa – 12,520, Guadalcanal – 7,100.")

(The flickers of light around her take tentative shape. They're foreign places? Monuments... Subway tunnels... Deserts... Buildings...)

WILL. I'll tell you what I *really* liked. And remember. Learning to code.

MATTY. That wasn't school though.

WILL. Nah. I learned on Logo Writer.

MATTY. Oh man you are *so old*. Did you learn on an Apple II? Are you that kid?

WILL. Logo was *awesome*. There was a turtle and his tail could draw things and if you got really good at it you could make him draw amazing stuff. I made him draw an animation of a shark eating a ninja. It took weeks. I was so proud of it.

...Wanting to learn isn't just about winning. It's about having a payoff for doing the work...

What if the exercises were part of like, a *quest*?

MATTY. A *quest*? Like – knights?

WILL. Like a *story*. Like – you're trying to defeat the evil – the evil –

MATTY. Zargons.

WILL.	**E-KAREN.**
– Prussians, but you can only do it if you build this catapult – which means that you need to measure the circumference of the wheels versus the wagon height versus the weight,	Need a hint? Now try it on your own.

WILL.	E-KAREN.
and then you need to learn to aim which means you need calculus...	You can do it. Try again.
And *then* you get to blow the Prussians up.	Log on tonight and try again.

WILL. I'd do it. I'd work that hard. In order to make something happen.

SANDY. Okay to put this in perspective – to this day – who's heard of a Purple Heart?

> (**JESSE** *raises his hand.*)

Shoshanna tell us what a Purple Heart is. Thank you. To this day, when a soldier is given a Purple Heart the actual medal was manufactured in 1945. Because the military placed such a large order, because they were convinced that that many people were about to die. Now Tanya will tell us a reason we shouldn't drop it.

Doesn't matter if you agree. Imagine – Truman has called you into the situation room and said – you tell me the pros, you tell me the cons.

Let's think about the documents we read for homework. The one about life in Tokyo...

They're running out of a bunch of things. Yes, good. Let's all listen while Cam reads paragraph five.

MATTY. What if it looked like a video game? What if every quest was set in a different world. And when you complete the quest, you move to a new world. Like say you're reading... Um. Fucking. Dickens.

E-KAREN. Welcome to London, 1848.

MATTY. You finish every question, every challenge, and you get to advance to a new world.

E-KAREN. Ready to visit Italy? There's a revolution going on.

MATTY. It's like – every day is a field trip.

Okay. You're not saying anything. It's a terrible idea.

WILL. No...

MATTY. It would be so much work.

WILL. *So* much work.

MATTY. And it would cost a ton of money.

WILL. A ton.

MATTY. We'd need to hire a whole graphics team.

WILL. ...It's the right thing to do.

SANDY. What if the Japanese were out of food, out of fuel, about to surrender, and we just leveled two of their cities, for no reason?

> (**JESSE** *raises his hand.*)

Jesse, yes!

JESSE. It seems like um. It seems like it comes down to what matters more, American or Japanese lives? And Truman picked American.

SANDY. Yeah. I guess – yeah, you could say that.

JESSE. That seems kind of screwed up.

SANDY. Maybe, yeah.

JESSE. Don't you think that's screwed up?

SANDY. I think you could make a case that it's the president's job to look after American lives. But you could make a case that the best way to look after American lives is to take care of foreign lives too.

JESSE. But what do *you* think? I don't see the point in like, on the one hand, on the other hand, wouldn't it be better to learn the *right* thing to do?

SANDY. There isn't always a right thing. One choice had one set of consequences and another had another.

> (*The bell rings.*)

Wait, wait wait – for homework – I want you to write a paragraph. What do *you* think should be a president's biggest priorities during war? I want you to support your argument with three specific examples. And what do I want to see? Right at the top of your paragraphs? A topic sentence! Amazing!

(Privately, to **JESSE.***)* I can't wait to hear what you have to say.

(**SANDY** *and* **JESSE** *exit.*)

(*The flickers of light have taken shape.* **WILL** *and* **MATTY** *are looking at – or standing in – a digital world. Like a screenshot from a video game. It's the New Mexico desert. And it's beautiful.*)

(*A title reads: "Welcome to Los Alamos, 1945."*)

WILL. Okay. I think the adaptive learning stuff is as good as it's gonna get.

E-KAREN. You seem to have trouble with group work. Why don't you try this level on your own.

WILL. Did we ever get the Spanish script back from that ODesk translator?

MATTY. I uploaded it an hour ago.

(*He types and the title changes to Spanish. He types again to change it back to English.*)

WILL. Okay...now...

(**MATTY** *hits a key to start the program.*)

E-KAREN. Find Truman's reasons for dropping the bomb in the answers below. A: troop shortages.

A: troop shortages.

A: troop shortages.

WILL. Jesus.

MATTY. Shit. Broke it.

WILL. Yeah.

MATTY. And the demo's on Friday.

WILL. Can you stay and look for the bug?

MATTY. You know ordinarily I'd be totally down to do that, but tonight I am actually supposed to go to a rave.

WILL. What?

MATTY. It's like a triphop dubstep mashup experience. In Richmond. You should come!

WILL. No thank you.

MATTY. I can help you tomorrow. Or at like six a.m.

WILL. No, no. It's alright. I'll take care of it. I just want to get it done.

> (**MATTY** *nods, leaves.*)
>
> (*The two apartments appear side by side.* **WILL** *goes home to his apartment, flops on the futon, and opens his laptop.*)
>
> (**ADAM** *enters his apartment, sits on his sofa, and watches a video on his phone.*)
>
> (**SANDY** *enters, kisses* **WILL** *on the forehead, and plunks down on the floor with a laptop.*)
>
> (**KAREN** *enters her apartment, sets down a set of papers, and gets to work with a red pen.*)
>
> (*They all stare at their glowing screens.* **SANDY**, **WILL**, *and* **ADAM** *wear headphones.*)

SANDY. (*Taking off her headphones.*) How was your day?

WILL. (*After a minute, removing his headphones.*) Huh?

SANDY. How was your day.

WILL. Um...

> (*Still typing. Finally looking up.*)

Good. It was good... It was hard actually.

SANDY. Oh...

> (*Realizing what he actually said.*)

Oh no! Are you okay?

WILL. Yeah, I'm fine.

> (**SANDY** *makes a nice face, then puts her headphones back in.*)

It just it still doesn't look as nice as I want it to and I hate the idea of anyone judging me based on work that *I know* isn't good enough –

SANDY. (*Taking headphones out.*) Huh?

WILL. Sorry. Never mind.

SANDY. No. It's fine.

WILL. No, it's not important.

(They both put their headphones back in.)

(ADAM laughs loudly.)

KAREN. What is it?

ADAM. *(Taking headphones out.)* Oh, it's stupid, it's just a video of a kangaroo pushing a guy into a river...
How was your day?

KAREN. It was good. How 'bout you?

ADAM. Pretty interesting.
Within the confines of being incredibly frustrating, since Mark is a jackass.

KAREN. Someday you'll have his job.

ADAM. Yeah but by then he'll probably have Jason's job and he'll still be my boss.

KAREN. I still think Jason's gonna get arrested for public exposure or something one of these days.

SANDY. Hanh said something really funny today.

WILL. *(Distracted by his screen.)* Yeah, totally...

(SANDY gives up and goes back to work.)

(ADAM gets up from the couch, goes to stand behind KAREN, massaging her neck.)

KAREN. Mmm. Oh wow.

(ADAM reads over her shoulder.)

ADAM. God that looks awful.

KAREN. Oh god it is. And then you get to ones like this –

(Holds one up.)

And you don't know whether to be depressed that they didn't even try, or just grateful that they made it so easy to grade.

ADAM. Do you ever think – maybe that idea Will had –

KAREN. No.

ADAM. It just seems like it could be helpful, in this circumstance?

KAREN. *No.* Baby – look here – this student is not checking her work. And this student – she's giving up. I don't just teach math. I teach organization. I teach hope. I teach that a black woman can have a socially conscious job, an engagement ring and a laser pointer, and that's an important lesson.

ADAM. You're right. I'm a moron.

KAREN. You know what he's building? Second-class education.

We know what works. Attention. Encouragement. We provide it for some kids.

But if you make something like that – a product that makes a bad system a little bit easier to live with – people won't demand a better system.

(Her phone rings. **ADAM** *hands it to her.)*

(On phone.) Hi Tiffany.

> *(She leaves the room.* **ADAM** *pulls one quiz from her pile and scrutinizes it.)*
>
> *(***SANDY** *takes out her headphones.)*

SANDY. We still haven't talked about the apartment.

WILL. What?

SANDY. I was just wondering whether maybe we should plan to look for a smaller apartment.

> *(***WILL** *sighs.)*

Or we could look in Oakland.

WILL. We don't have to move to Oakland.

SANDY. I'd have a shorter commute.

It's just that we have to either renew the lease or not by the end of the month.

WILL. I don't want to talk about it now. You know I have the demo on Friday.

SANDY. Okay but the rent is going up by 300 –

WILL. I know that.

SANDY. And my salary's definitely not going up by that much. And we don't know what's going to happen with yours –

WILL. I just can't talk about it now, okay? I can't worry about these little things, I have something to do.

> (**SANDY** *suppresses her temper, starts to head out.*)

SANDY. Just FYI...you are not the only person who has important stuff to do tomorrow.

> (*She goes.* **WILL** *sits, annoyed and guilty.*)

> (**KAREN** *comes back in.*)

KAREN. Easy homework question.

> (*She picks up her tests and resumes grading.*)

ADAM. Are you going to have much grading this weekend?

KAREN. I've got three more classes of these.

ADAM. What if we went to Napa.

Or Big Sur. I would go to Big Sur. No, I think Napa. We can eat at the Spicy Cow, or whatever it's called.

KAREN. The Salty Pig.

ADAM. We can eat at the Salty Pig.

KAREN. Where's this coming from?

ADAM. Nowhere. I'm just – I'm sick of work. They're on my back every second – come in early, stay until midnight. It's not like we're neurosurgeons or something! We're not doing anything important. We're – gamblers. I just want to have a couple days of fun. Find a place with an outdoor hot tub. Get massages... Read a book?

KAREN. ...But if we go to Napa...we will get drunk –

ADAM. Yes.

KAREN. And I will not be able to grade or plan a single thing.

ADAM. *Exactly.*

I have a theory...that a person can be both good, and happy. Now unfortunately I can't test my theory because I'm not a good enough person. But you could test it.

You get to be happy, Kare.

KAREN. Well when you put it like that.

ADAM. Are you in?

KAREN. I'm in.

ADAM. Yes! Awesome! Let's pick out a hotel before you change your mind.

> (**KAREN**'s cell phone rings. She picks up.)

KAREN. (On phone.) Hi Jesse.

> (She exits.)

> (**SANDY** enters in a t-shirt and boxers.)

SANDY. I'm going to sleep.

WILL. I'm sorry. I was stupid.

> (**SANDY** walks over to him. She puts her toes over his toes.)

> (He looks up. Puts a toe over one of her toes. They stay like that for a moment.)

SANDY. I have work at five, so...

WILL. I get it. I'll just be a little while longer.

> (**SANDY** kisses the top of his head and leaves.)

> (**WILL** keeps going in his bright light.)

Scene Five

(Five months later. The bar in Oakland.)

KAREN. So everyone finally approved the invitation wording.

SANDY. Fifth draft?

KAREN. Seventh. Eighth.

SANDY. How about the uh – about the prenup stuff?

KAREN. Oh, that's all settled.

SANDY. So you did end up...

KAREN. Oh, you know it's really – it's a legal formality – it's not something *he's* concerned about, it's to keep his father happy, and I understand that. I would be that protective with my kids. And I may have traded signing it for having the final say in where the kids go for school, church and Christmas.

SANDY. Ha! Nice.

KAREN. It's not exactly legally enforceable but I think it sets a nice precedent of total control.

SANDY. Absolutely.

KAREN. I'm so glad you came out this week! You have broken the sacred Friday tradition / so many times this semester –

SANDY. I know I'm the worst. I'm the absolute worst.

KAREN. I heard you've been staying till nine.

SANDY. Not *nine*.

KAREN. Deborah said she saw you leaving after the hall lights shut off last week.

SANDY. Well that means Deborah was there after the lights went off.

KAREN. She forgot her house keys.

SANDY. Right. Yeah I guess I didn't think Deborah was staying to help people.

KAREN. *Nine* Sandy.

SANDY. I'm trying to have one-on-one conferences about their essays.

KAREN. Burnout is a real thing.

SANDY. You know about Janelle?

KAREN. Is she alright?

SANDY. She's moving to Denver. Her husband got a promotion.

KAREN. ...You want to be the next head of the history department.

SANDY. I was wondering what it was like when your department went through it.

KAREN. Is that why you're finally getting drinks with me??

SANDY. No. Don't be stupid.

KAREN. I'm useless anyways.

It was only our second year, I tried to stay out of it.

SANDY. But you must have been keeping an eye on it for – y'know. Future reference...

KAREN. Sandy... I'm leaving once I have kids.

I'm gonna take a couple years. Figure out the next thing. I don't know what yet. Graduate school. Nonprofit work. You know my parents have always been disappointed that I'm not a lawyer.

SANDY. But –

I thought we were lifers.

KAREN. This job is impossible. It's impossible. They want more from us every year, and they give us less and less resources to deal with it. And instead of standing up and saying, "That's not alright. If you value kids you will invest in them." We say, "Okay, I guess I'll do more." I can feel myself getting too tired to do this properly.

You know what I found out this week? I have a student who's been falling asleep in class. Turns out his mom got evicted and for the last year he's been sleeping on his aunt's couch in Fairfield and taking the bus two hours every morning to get to school.

SANDY. Jesus.

KAREN. What miracle am I supposed to work so that everything's okay for that kid? I can't fix something that everyone else in the country just lets happen.

SANDY. Who is it?

KAREN. Jesse Connell.

SANDY. Oh god. God. I taught him last semester. I used to nag him about getting tired in class! He wrote a really good final paper on Vietnam.

KAREN. And how many hours of after-school help did that take?

Look this isn't Dead Poets Society, if you want to be department head you've got to play the game.

SANDY. How did you guys pick Allen?

KAREN. He had the highest test scores for a lot of years running. It felt objective, you know?

Numbers showed he was the best.

SANDY. Objective evidence. That makes sense.

What else?

KAREN. He was like you, really dedicated, in before school, after school. But he wasn't too opinionated Sandy, he went easy on the other people in the department.

SANDY. I can go easy on people.

KAREN. And he had a clear plan for how the rest of the department could get their scores up.

(*Beat.*)

SANDY. I can have a plan.

(*The startup office.* **MATTY** *is on the phone.* **WILL** *watches* **MATTY** *and listens.*)

MATTY. (*On phone.*) So you've just taught Newton's First Law. And a kid logs in and boom! He's on a spaceship! And he has to like use Newton's law to navigate a – a fucking – asteroid field. Using orbits. And stuff.

Oh right, of course. Dinnertime, yeah, get going. Get yourself some meatloaf.

We'll catch up. How 'bout tomorrow?

Yeah we'll catch up soon. And a good evening to you as well!

WILL. You can't say / fucking.

MATTY. I know.

WILL. On a call with a high school administrator!

Have you ever tried "um" as a placeholder in your sentences?

MATTY. Meh.

So I don't know if you've noticed this, but man. Working in education is like, a fucking, I don't want to say panty melter because that's trite, but I will say it is a heart melter. That also works on panties. Like you say, "I'm just looking for a way to help America's kids," and they're like, "Really? Wow? You think kids matter?"

I mean it's great cuz, I don't think it works with male teachers, cuz they're just teachers, you know, but we are like, men who care about kids *and* money. Aka, negligee solvents. I'm not implying that I think dissolving is the same chemical process as melting / believe me, I know the difference.

WILL. Oh my god, shut up, shut the fucking fuck up!

Stop swearing on work calls, stop talking about panties, stop stop stop stop stop. No.

MATTY. Dude.

I'm going to give you some privacy so you can remove the rabid squirrel from your butt.

WILL. The state of California just changed the English reading list.

MATTY. Oh. Okay. So – so –

WILL. So we are sitting on dozens of modules we can't use and we have to pay people to come back in and make dozens of new ones.

MATTY. Please at least tell me that they cut The Scarlet Letter.

WILL. And if we hire people, we go from having a four-month runway to having a three-week runway.

MATTY. Three weeks, we can do a lot in three weeks.

WILL. No we can't.

MATTY. We could stop drawing salaries, buy ourselves some time.

WILL. You can do that?

MATTY. For a couple months, yeah.

WILL. ...I can't do that.

MATTY. We could bring out some units before the whole curriculum is ready.

WILL. That seems shitty. And haphazard.

MATTY. Can your parents lend us money?

WILL. My parents run a Subway franchise in Stockton.

MATTY. Can they get us free sandwiches?

WILL. Matty!

MATTY. We could ask your buddy to do another seed round. Or we could drink three Red Bulls and do the new modules ourselves. Tonight.

I'm great at fucking literary analysis.

WILL. You sound like a five-year-old. You are laughing at real problems.

MATTY. Because if you treat them like they're problems, you're not gonna solve them! All you're gonna see is problems. But if you treat it like it's fun, like it's a game, maybe you have a shot at actually having a legit new idea.

WILL. Or maybe you'll just blow a good sales lead!

MATTY. We could run ads.

WILL. We have a three-week runway and you want to blow it on advertising?

Can you do math? Or sales? Or strategy?

Or anything besides just crack jokes and dissolve fucking panties?

MATTY. You know what? Maybe you should have founded this five years ago.

Maybe you would still have had some guts.

Instead of just like sinking testosterone levels and student loans.

WILL. You are a moron alright? You are a community college dropout. You would be a mediocre dime a dozen brogrammer if I hadn't happened to choose you to do something special. I want you to remember that, and I want you to get out of here.

MATTY. Seriously?

WILL. Get out of here!

> (MATTY *starts to leave. When he's halfway out, he turns back to throw the basketball as hard as he can at* WILL.)

> (*It misses and hits the desk instead, ricochets off.* MATTY *scatters papers and leaves.*)

> (WILL *is left alone. Maybe he rubs his shoulders, or his eyes. He deals with the toll a long day takes on the human body.*)

> (*Projections fade up on the surfaces around him. At first it's beautiful – a digital rendition of a historic city. Then its underlying architecture fades in – the geometric forms that make up the image; the walls of Ruby code. The endless work under the beauty.*)

> (SANDY *enters, carrying bags of takeout.*)

SANDY. Hey!! I brought takeout.

WILL. Oh. Thanks.

SANDY. Don't be too excited.

What's wrong?

WILL. I'm so tired.

> (SANDY *goes to sit in his lap. He rests his head on her shoulder. She puts her arms around him.*)

SANDY. Poor Wilbur.

WILL. Don't call me that.

SANDY. It's your name.

WILL. Which is something no one ever needs to know.

SANDY. What's wrong?

WILL. I pissed Matty off.

SANDY. Have you ever heard of a company where the cofounders didn't have fights?

WILL. No, but –

SANDY. Do you think he's about to quit?

WILL. Probably not.

SANDY. Then you're fine.

WILL. I'm not fine.

Our English section is out of date.

Our reports page keeps breaking.

I think our lawyer sucks but I don't have time to find a new one.

We blew all this money on graphics, and now I don't have any to pay for product testing, and without it we can't be market-ready, and if we're not market-ready, we can't make money to pay for more graphics.

I don't know if I can do this. I'm not good enough.

SANDY. You are.

WILL. No, I'm not. Here's the proof.

SANDY. What if I tested it in my classroom?

(**WILL** *isn't sure what to say.*)

I mean, it's not a huge sample size, but, 215 kids, you'd get a sense really quickly of what's working and what's not.

WILL. We're not totally ready with all of the history – other subjects have more questions.

SANDY. I can talk to other teachers. To the school. I mean, even if there's only – one who wants to try it, in each department, that's still –

WILL. 200-plus testers.

SANDY. *(Gets up, goes to the computer.)* It runs on Windows tablets right?

WILL. The new ones, yeah.

SANDY. And it's integrated with state textbook chapters.
That's good. I can sell that. I can sell that to lazy teachers.
Is the parent login working yet?

WILL. I'd like to marry you.

SANDY. What?

WILL. We've talked about it. And I think now.

SANDY. You think now.

WILL. Yeah. Before I thought, get my PhD first, then I
thought get the company off the ground first but I
don't care anymore.

SANDY. You want to get engaged?

WILL. Yes. That's what I meant.

SANDY. And the wording you picked was, "We already
agreed, and I think now"?

WILL. Why does it matter how we get engaged, what matters
is we'll be engaged.
I don't have to say it in some great way, for it to be a
good thing.
It will be a good thing.

(Beat. Then **SANDY** *kisses him.)*

SANDY. You're right.

WILL. I mean. I can write down some nicer stuff to say for
when we have like a ring and a restaurant reservation
and everything.

SANDY. I've actually – I've never wanted a ring.

WILL. Really?

SANDY. Yeah. I think they're – a lot of stuff. Materialistic,
patriarchal, bad for Africa...

WILL. So. Does that mean. So are we engaged now?

SANDY. Yeah, I think we are.

WILL. Fuck.

*(***SANDY*** hits him. He kisses her.)*

I'm happy.
Are you happy?

SANDY. I'm happy.
WILL. Are you happy?
SANDY. I'm really happy.

ACT TWO

Scene One

(Two months later. **WILL** *and* **ADAM** *are in Karen and Adam's apartment.)*

ADAM. How does one arrange cheese?

WILL. I don't know.

ADAM. Come on, you have design experience.

WILL. Okay. You arrange cheese in a user-friendly way, with a clear call to action above the fold.

ADAM. I suppose one could think of the fig jam as a call to action.

WILL. Yeah that looks great.

ADAM. Would you like any cheese?

WILL. I'm lactose intolerant.

ADAM. Hey, so uh – did you hear about the new artificial intelligence funding –

WILL. For the Open AI initiative? Yes! Yes!! How did you hear about that?

ADAM. I may have started reading Hacker News.
So you think it's a good thing?

WILL. It's amazing. I'm so afraid that I'm going to die before we've made a general AI. If people are putting money into it then maybe we'll get to it fast enough and I get to see it.

ADAM. But I mean – come on, you have to be a little worried about like intelligent killer robots.

WILL. I don't see why everyone harps on that.

ADAM. Skynet...Terminator...Blade Runner...

WILL. Dude, that's like the least interesting thing about AI. Come on – *superintelligence*. Calm, objective superintelligence with unlimited analytical power. It could comb through all the data in the world, and write laws for us that are actually the best laws to pass. It could tell us what taxes to have, what wars to get into or avoid. It could invent things for us. Jetpacks. Microsurgery. Supercheese. Shit we can't even imagine.

ADAM. It does seem a little sad though. Isn't it fun figuring it out for ourselves?

WILL. It's not fun. It's horrible. We screw up so badly all the time and it has these huge huge consequences. I think someday every part of our lives will be better.

ADAM. That seems pretty utopian.

WILL. Why not? We have vaccines. We can get to Beijing in twelve hours. Life is 500 times better than it's ever been before. Why assume that it can't get 500 times better again?

(**SANDY** *and* **KAREN** *enter with takeout bags.*)

SANDY. Fish tacos in the house!

WILL. How'd it go? I've been texting!

ADAM. *(To* **KAREN**.*)* Hey Ms. Green.

KAREN. Hey.

(**ADAM** *kisses her.*)

SANDY. I never answer texts while I'm driving, it's irresponsible.

WILL. So?

ADAM. Sandy, how does one arrange cheese?

SANDY. Appetizingly? Horizontally.

WILL. *What happened????*

SANDY. They went for it!

WILL. Yeah?

SANDY. And – Ron said that kind of thinking showed real leadership potential.

(**WILL** *grabs* **SANDY**, *hugs her, spins her around.*)

ADAM. Ahh, young love.

WILL. Yes! Yes!

ADAM. Can I hear what this is about so I can help celebrate?

WILL. Their school's gonna be our first client!

ADAM. That's great! Way to go man.

> *(He hugs* **WILL.***)*

> *(To* **KAREN.***)* I know you have some reservations about it, I'm just happy for a friend.

> *(Weird, slight pause.)*

KAREN. Yeah. Of course.

WILL. Honestly, it's so different from when we talked about it –

KAREN. No, yeah, I got to hear all about it from Sandy's presentation. It sounds really impressive.

WILL. Yeah?

KAREN. Yeah!

Congratulations.

ADAM. Fuck beer, I'm getting champagne!

> *(He exits.)*

SANDY. Champagne and fish tacos. Not bad for a Wednesday night.

WILL. *(To* **KAREN.***)* I'm glad you like the idea now.

KAREN. It sounds like all you boys are onto something.

WILL. We are. We *are*.

> (**ADAM** *enters with a bottle and champagne flutes.*)

ADAM. Karen's mom says that if you don't keep champagne in the fridge that means you don't think you deserve to have anything good happen to you.

SANDY. Reason eight hundred and eleven why I love your mother.

ADAM. Well I would like to propose a toast – oh damn I started saying that early and now I have all this unwrapping to do. Okay, eloquence! I would like to propose a toast to my stunningly brilliant friends, to their engagement, which deserves to be celebrated again, and to their professional triumphs, which we get to celebrate for the first time and oh thank god – okay, everybody get a glass – to love, to happiness, and to success – cheers.

SANDY. Cheers!

>   (*Everyone clinks.*)

ADAM. To – remind me the company's name?

SANDY. Personal Classroom!

ADAM. To Personal Classroom. And to Will's success!

KAREN. And yours.

ADAM. Hmm?

KAREN. Did you not tell Will about the promotion?

ADAM. Oh, yeah, that's nothing.

SANDY. You got promoted?

ADAM. I mostly got like a, congrats, you've been here three years and haven't been fired so your title's changed thing?

SANDY. To Adam not being fired!

WILL. Cheers.

KAREN. Cheers.

And to Sandy too. She gives a hell of a presentation.

ADAM. We all know Sandy is very good at talking.

SANDY. Quality *and* quantity.

ADAM. No seriously, I remember you doing some kind of – I don't know – activism in college, you were amazing. I was ready to sponsor a palm schoolhouse in Nicaragua or whatever it was.

KAREN. But also, so thorough, she had screenshots, she had FAQs... She had testimonials from students!

ADAM. Wow.

SANDY. I think that was a little cheesy.

KAREN. People were impressed. And she'd thought of everything. Right at the end she was like, "I want to be completely open and forthright, I do have an interest in this. This program was designed by my fiancé. And the principal investor is the fiancé of another teacher, Karen Green."

ADAM. Okay. Okay.

SANDY. Yeah, I mean, I didn't want people to find out later, and say I hadn't been aboveboard about the whole thing.

KAREN. Good call.

ADAM. Well it all sounds – very professional. Good job Sandy. Tacos?

(He pulls boxes of food from the takeout bags.)

KAREN. Hey Will – just out of curiosity – how much did Adam invest?

| **ADAM.** | **WILL.** |
| Karen – | What? |

KAREN. Just because apparently he doesn't tell me anything, and I can't trust the number he'll tell me later so I'd rather just hear it from you.

(Everyone freezes.)

ADAM. Karen maybe we can do this later?

KAREN. No. Because I have already been publicly embarrassed twice today and if I can handle it you can too.

Do you want to say anything?

ADAM. What do you want me to say?

KAREN. You could start with I'm sorry.

ADAM. I'm sorry. I'm sorry that I didn't tell you. But I did think of you. I think this will make your job a lot easier –

KAREN. You think lying to me will make my job easier?

ADAM. I didn't lie.

KAREN. No, you ignored me.

ADAM. I didn't –

KAREN. You are a careless person. You just say yes to everybody / without thinking about what's right.

ADAM. I have my own opinions. I'm allowed to.

KAREN. We are getting married, you don't just get to do whatever you want –

ADAM. It's my money!

>(**KAREN** *stares at him for a moment.*)

KAREN. Excuse me.

>(*She exits.*)

>(**ADAM** *takes a step after her and turns back.*)

ADAM. I'm sorry guys. Maybe we can...

SANDY.	**WILL.**
Yeah we're gonna head out.	Yeah...

>(**WILL** *and* **SANDY** *head back to their place. They sit side by side on the futon.*)

WILL. What other questions did they have?

SANDY. Um. There were some about keeping student records safe.

WILL. You knew how to answer those.

SANDY. They loved the problems though, some teachers were trying to solve them during the presentation.

WILL. Nice.

That's awesome that Ron said that about leadership potential.

You should be running that school.

SANDY. So you really didn't know he hadn't told her?

WILL. I told you, we never talked about it.

SANDY. Of course you didn't. Boys.

WILL. I assumed he had. It seemed awkward so I never brought it up.

SANDY. ...Do you think you should give the money back?

WILL. What?

We've already spent most of the money.

SANDY. Well whatever's left of it.

WILL. No. That's – that's pulling the plug.

SANDY. It just feels like we shouldn't have it. I mean, they're basically paying our *rent*, and she never agreed –

WILL. No they aren't –

SANDY. I don't want to take sides –

WILL. I'm just stating a fact. Look Adam didn't give me the money as a *present*. He made an investment. You don't give back an investment, you use it.

Sandy we're close. The product looks great. Adam did something stupid it was so bad and stupid –

SANDY. God how could he be so stupid.

WILL. But it's done. And we have a chance to do something awesome.

Your school's into it. We already have interest from a couple other schools for next year. You know there've been times when I've thought this was crazy. It's crazy. But it's also not. At the Petwork workspace, one of the guys was building a company that sends you a box of razors every month. They just got a six hundred million dollar valuation. They aren't even doing something cool. This could totally happen. It's not unreasonable to hope for – low end, a hundred million dollar acquisition. Just a hundred mil. It could happen. It's not that much.

SANDY. And yet it is also a lot.

WILL. Cuz then, my share after taxes is fifteen million. If you invest that properly, you get a steady income of 400,000 a year. Have some security. Some flexibility.

SANDY. Buy an apartment.

WILL. Buy my parents a house that isn't shitty.

SANDY. You know what I'd want?

WILL. What?

SANDY. A Winnebago.

WILL. Really?

SANDY. Absolutely. I've only been to twenty-seven states. You could take a couple years off, right, or take it a little easier at work? What if we spent every summer cruising around in a Winnebago.

WILL. We could eat our way across America.

I would also really like to buy a drone.

SANDY. And it would be cool to be able to give like actual amounts of money to charity. Instead of like, here's your ten dollars for the year.

WILL. Yeah.

Of course, if it went for, say...five *billion*...

If my share was a billion dollars. You could found a charity. Support whatever you want.

SANDY. Buy a three-bedroom apartment...

WILL. And *two* Winnebagos.

SANDY. We could drag race Winnebagos.

> (**WILL** *kisses her. Her cell phone dings – a text message. It dings again. She finds it –*)

Karen called off the wedding.

> (*The startup office.*)

> (**ADAM** *is looking over a printout.* **WILL** *and* **MATTY** *come in, watch* **ADAM**. *They fidget.*)

> (**SANDY** *exits.* **ADAM** *turns a page.*)

WILL. *What do you think?*

ADAM. You're not growing fast enough.

WILL. I mean. With an enterprise startup initial growth is usually a lot slower.

You don't *want* a lot of people trying it until the product is refined.

ADAM. You're not going to get a next round of investment unless you're growing exponentially.

That's it. Other companies are.

You have – what – three schools using it now?

MATTY. Three and a half.

ADAM. And you're not even charging them?

WILL. You get the users in first, then when they're addicted, you charge. That's the way it works.

ADAM. But – three. Is nothing.

MATTY. Three and a half. Rounds up.

WILL. It's hard to make an institutional sale.

There's a lot more bureaucracy. A food chain.

Charter schools have been interested, but – I mean real approval for a major change should come from at least a superintendent. Ideally a city government.

MATTY. Not to mention principals and superintendents are gutless pricks. You say, like, experiment, high-tech and their balls shrivel up.

ADAM. So don't say those words.

MATTY. Well I know that *now*.

ADAM. ...Hire me.

MATTY. Wait. You mean like –

ADAM. As a salesperson.

WILL. Are things not going well at the fund?

ADAM. No. Things are great. I'm just – I'm sick of it.

WILL. Well you don't have to work.

MATTY. What are your sales qualifications?

WILL. I think it could be very uncomfortable having an investor who isn't a co-founder working at the company.

ADAM. *The principle* investor –

WILL. See it's that, it's comments like that –

ADAM. You owe me this.

I am not losing my fiancée –

WILL. You lost your fiancée / because of your own –

ADAM. – For the sake of a company that *fails*.

WILL. We're *not* failing.

It is not my fault that you were a shitty boyfriend.

ADAM. Are you fucking kidding?

MATTY. Just FYI, I wasn't kidding when I asked about your sales qualifications.

ADAM. I'm a likable person.

MATTY. I think that's really for us to judge.

ADAM. I'm better than a fucking geek.

MATTY. Not proving your point.

WILL. We're working on it. We know we need to refine our sales pitch, and we've been making progress.

ADAM. Will. Half of the people you talk to, you piss off.
My father knows a lot of important people.

WILL. *Wow*, you want to play that card?

ADAM. Yeah. I do. So should you. Mayors. State congressmen.
You need them. You need me.

So you know what, I'm not saying anything else.

I'm waiting for you to ask.

> *(He exits.)*

MATTY. ...I liked him.

WILL. He doesn't know anything about coding. Or graphics.
Or UI. We'd have to explain god damn everything to
him.

"I know so many senators and billionaires. The mayor
of West Whifflepuff? Of course! His son and I were polo
rivals!"

MATTY. I thought you were hungry, man.

There is no proud in hungry.

WILL. That sounds like a really weird, depressing t-shirt.

MATTY. What is life, but a really weird depressing t-shirt?

> *(They exit.* **ADAM** *appears on the phone, pacing.)*

ADAM. *(On phone.)* Hi! James. It's Adam. Tripp's son.

Great, he said you'd be expecting it.

Yeah, I actually wanted to talk because I've gone into
business! So exciting.

Well, it's in the EdTech sector, and I was wondering
whether you might still have some contacts from the
mayoral years.

Oh god no, we're not looking to make any sales yet,
we're still in the beta stage. We're just hoping to get
some advice, understand the market's needs.

That would be amazing! Sure, I'll email Shirley. And
then you'll have my info in case you think of anyone
else.

No, those ones sound amazing, thanks so much.

You too, you too. Yeah, maybe in Kennebunkport!

(He hangs up, moves to the couch, dials.)

Hey Heather!

Oh my god, I know, I can't believe how long it's been. I saw your birthday on Facebook and I was like, holy crap it's been so long. It's your fault for not coming to reunion.

No way. Columbia Teachers College is – an amazing school. That's actually – that's so weird, I'm actually kind of in the same field now.

No, no more finance.

Well it's cool, it's – you know what? I'm gonna be in New York in two weeks for my mom's birthday, we should catch up.

I would *love* that. Nah, Karen won't be in town. School calendar.

She says hi back.

Yeah. Looking forward to it!

(He hangs up. Can't go on for a moment.)

(He snaps back into it. Dials.)

Scene Two

(Four months later. **SANDY** *sits at her teacher's desk, dressed in an eighties outfit.)*

*(***JESSE*** *enters. He's dressed differently now, more confidently. He fidgets less.)*

JESSE. Um. Ms. Friedman?

SANDY. Hey Jesse! Hi. How are you doing?

JESSE. Pretty good. Yeah.

(Of her costume.) Reagan day?

SANDY. It's totally tubular.

JESSE. Honestly I'm kind of amazed you're not dressed like Sandra Day O'Connor.

SANDY. That is an awesome idea.

How's senior year?

JESSE. Um. Fun. Sometimes. Hard. But in a good way.

SANDY. Good.

Do you want to um – want to take a seat?

JESSE. Sure, yeah. Thanks.

So – um. So Ms. Green suggested I should come talk to you. You guys are friends, right?

SANDY. Yeah. Good friends.

JESSE. So I'm, ah – I'm actually looking at colleges. And I'm looking for a place with a good history department.

SANDY. Oh! Wow.

JESSE. Yeah. Yeah so I had Ms. Green last year, and she talked a lot about, about like, figuring out what you're actually mad at, you know? Or like, figuring out what's worth getting mad at? And she said, you have to get yourself into a position where you can take those big things on.

SANDY. That's great advice. I'm so glad you want to study history.

JESSE. Yeah. I mean, I don't want to study "history" like, what was the tariff of eighteenwhatever. I want to study political science. I think I want to be a community organizer.

SANDY. I think that's *so. Great.*

JESSE. ...And Ms. Green said I should get a letter of recommendation from a history teacher. And I've been doing a lot better this year. But for history I had Welker, and he was – he still gets me confused with Lamar.

SANDY. Oh god, yeah. He's um –

JESSE. He sucks.

SANDY. Between you and me? Yeah. He does.

JESSE. So can you like fire him now that you're head of the department?

SANDY. Sadly no. But I can nag him a lot.

JESSE. Look I know we didn't always get along super well? But I liked your class. By the end. A lot.

And I feel like – you know me pretty well. And like – you've seen what can happen when I'm trying. So I was wondering whether you feel like maybe you're the right person to write a letter for me.

SANDY. Absolutely.

JESSE. Yeah?

SANDY. Of course. I'd be happy to.

JESSE. That's great. That's great.

SANDY. Obviously, you know, get me the list, the dates for everything. As soon as you can.

JESSE. Yup, yes, right.

SANDY. And um – you know, if you need any advice about programs – or the application process. I'll be here.

JESSE. Great. I'm sure I will. I should – for now I have to get to work.

SANDY. Sure, sure.

(**JESSE** *starts to go.*)

Hey Jesse – I have a class for seniors. On modern culture. If you're interested.

JESSE. Yeah. That sounds cool.

SANDY. Oh, and, um – if you haven't done it already? I think you should write Ms. Green a thank you card.

JESSE. That's a great idea. Yeah. I'll do that. Look, um – thanks.

SANDY. No problem.

> (**JESSE** *waves and goes.*)
>
> (*The startup office. Late at night.* **WILL** *and* **ADAM** *are there, maybe having beers.*)

ADAM. The principal of Harding Prep. The number two at KIPP.

The *mayor of Fresno*.

They all say the same thing: what if a kid runs out of questions?

WILL. We have literally thousands of questions.

ADAM. But what if a kid *keeps* getting questions right, they're bored, they're ready to move on...

WILL. That's a different problem. Can you be more specific when you talk?

ADAM. Or what if they need to review something. If they keep getting certain questions wrong.

WILL. They get easier questions.

ADAM. But if they're just not getting something. Even the easy questions.

WILL. They wait for a teacher to come help them.

ADAM. But the teacher's over on the other side of the room, helping another kid with a different thing he isn't getting.

You haven't taken the burden off teachers. You've created a nightmare where thirty different kids are working on thirty different things and the teacher has to scurry between them doing one-on-one lessons. And in the meantime while they're waiting for the teacher the kids are on their phones, they're falling asleep, they distract other students. It's chaos!

WILL. So, what are you saying.

Are you saying it's fatally flawed or something?

Are you saying it doesn't work?

ADAM. Matty had one potential idea / which I think is really good –

WILL. You already talked about this with Matty?

ADAM. We were both in the office one night. You had a thing with Sandy.

What if we had lessons? Videos.

The program notices you missed five questions in a row about...metaphors, it suggests you watch a helpful short video on what a metaphor is.

WILL. Are you suggesting – that's insane. That's an insane number of videos.

ADAM. Yup. A short video explaining every basic concept in math, science, English, history, available on demand for every student at the exact moment they're ready for it. The software shouldn't be a supplement, or a review tool. It should be a complete education.

WILL. I mean that's – that's crazy. That's so much –

The *server* space alone –

ADAM. Will is that really your biggest thought, oh no we'd need an awful lot of server space?

WILL. I don't think teachers will go for it.

ADAM. Are you worried that teachers won't go for it, or that your girlfriend won't go for it?

WILL. It's a problem – it's a real problem – if a department head doesn't like the software they won't get their team on board.

ADAM. Unless the principal likes the software.

WILL. You floated this already with Sandy's principal?

ADAM. I'm your client relations manager.

I went out for drinks with a client. To get his thoughts.

And he's thinking he may not use the software next year if it stays the way it is. But he thought that if it had videos, that would be something he would pay for.

WILL. I have to think about it.

ADAM. If you don't do it, you don't have a company Will. You have a joke.

WILL. I don't know yet. I have to think.

ADAM. ...You know when I met you...obviously I knew who you were, I'd seen you around at freshman orientation. But – Jamie and Roberto and I were in my common room, talking about BitTorrent. Talking through how it worked. And all of a sudden this guy wanders in. Wearing a fucking Halo shirt.

And your opening words were, "You're getting it wrong." I thought – what kind of person cares so little about popularity, or shyness, or fear, and *all* he cares about is the right answer.

That's a person worth being around. There's so much power in a person like that.

> *(He leaves. **SANDY** appears in the background in her apartment.)*

SANDY. And what would I be doing, while they were watching the videos?

> *(**WILL** reluctantly gets up. Goes home.)*

WILL. Supervising.

SANDY. Supervising...

WILL. You'd make sure they were focused. See if they were having any problems.

SANDY. But I wouldn't *teach*.

WILL. Their content learning would come from a combination of videos and articles. So every student could learn what they were ready for on their own timeline. A lot of studies say student-directed learning is the most effective / style of pedagogy –

SANDY. Damn it I *told* you that! I fed you that line.

WILL. It's not a line. This is what we talked about. Personalized teaching.

SANDY. Videos aren't *teaching*.

The teachers' union won't go for it. Just for starters.

WILL. Well I think petticoat manufacturers were probably pretty upset when petticoats went out of fashion, but that doesn't mean we should all walk around wearing them just to keep them happy.

SANDY. You think this is a good idea.

WILL. I think *maybe* it's a good idea. I think it's an idea worth exploring.

SANDY. No, look – learning is personal, alright? If good content were all it took for kids to learn then we wouldn't need schools just *libraries* –

WILL. I've thought about that and I have some ideas –

SANDY. Can you listen?

Making someone learn is *hard*. You have to get to know kids, you forge a connection.

You entertain them, you encourage them, you guide them –

WILL. *You* do. Not everyone does.

I've heard you talk about the bad teachers. I *had* bad teachers.

In eighth grade I had a science teacher who was really a home-ec teacher, but she'd been at the school longer and when home-ec got dropped she had seniority and she didn't know *anything*. And my dad worked with me every night, for an hour, to teach me all the stuff she wasn't / teaching.

SANDY. That's the exception –

WILL. You know why I never liked history? I had a history teacher my junior year, who told me that "my people" were a bunch of robotic grade grubbers, and she gave me Cs for a year to "build my character."

Even the good ones...

Do you never screw up? Do you never get a fact wrong? Do you never play favorites?

SANDY. Of course I'm not perfect. No one is perfect, um you're not either by the way –

WILL. Kids learning things on their own timeline. Is that really so terrible?

All kids having access to good lessons. The same lessons. In Oakland, or in Marin. In Manhattan, or the Bronx, or South Dakota. Come on, I mean take a minute, imagine this with me... Couldn't it be kind of cool?

SANDY. *No.* I have two master's degrees. I have six years of experience. I am not a checkout bagger, you cannot automate what I do.

WILL. Okay so tell me, explain it to me. What about it doesn't work?

SANDY. You just want to talk me out of what I think.

WILL. No, I want to understand what's wrong with it.

SANDY. *Everything's* wrong with it.

> (**WILL** *waits.*)

What if the students have questions?

Or ideas they want to explore? Kids need people to talk to! They need to learn to talk to adults, they need to learn to talk to each other, they need –

WILL. Slow down, slow down...

SANDY. I mean, who's going to help them with papers? How do papers work?

Kids need to do hands-on work. They need to unplug and do something physical. It's good for memory, it's good for developing social skills –

WILL. Okay. Okay! So what if –

What if when two kids both finish the same problems, the system pairs them up? And gives them a physical assignment?

> (**E-KAREN** *appears. Maybe there's something a little different about her this time. Maybe her appearance is more human.*)

E-KAREN. You've both studied weights, mass, and forces... meet at the back of the class to build a pulley strong enough to lift your desk.

SANDY. Well that's... That's complicated. That kind of work is messy.

A teacher would need to be like, getting the materials set up. And stepping in if some of the kids were being assholes.

WILL. Sure, sure. But that's great! The teacher has time to help, because her other students are busy with the videos.

SANDY. Maybe.

WILL. What would make it – I know you'd miss the content teaching.

But what would make it something you'd be *excited* about?

If you didn't have to waste time reviewing facts with them. What would you be able to do?

SANDY. Collaborative work. Creative work.

E-KAREN. Record three radio advertisements to air during Roosevelt's fireside chat.

SANDY. Critical thinking stuff. Not just facts but, analysis.

E-KAREN. Design an experiment to test your theory.

SANDY. Independent projects. Kids need to learn how to pursue a goal, how to break it down into steps. And they need to talk it through with a grownup! To hang out with an adult, who can say, this is how you do stuff, this is how you be an adult in the world.

WILL. We can make that happen. Okay so imagine –

Any given minute twenty kids are on their computers, yes – but ten kids at a time are rehearsing a skit...or solving a problem set. Or meeting with a teacher.

E-KAREN. Come to the front of the room and check in about your paper.

SANDY. That might work. It might work.

WILL. And everything would be during the school day. You could be home at five.

SANDY. You might not get a fight from the teachers' unions. If you're employing just as many teachers, and just – letting them focus on the best parts of the job.

WILL. How would you feel about – I don't know, but. When the school year ends – you could come work with us. Be a curriculum advisor. Director of pedagogy.

SANDY. I'd –

I'd miss my students.

WILL. You'd have millions of students.

(Beat. **SANDY** *is undeniably tempted.)*

Scene Three

*(**JESSE**'s in the classroom – but the classroom now looks like the startup office. He's on an iPad, wearing headphones.)*

*(**SANDY** sits at the teacher's desk and watches her students, watching their tablets.)*

*(Stillness. Silence. **SANDY** just watches.)*

SANDY. Try turning it off and then on again, Gabbie.

(She may get up to walk through the classroom, checking screens. The kids are working. There's nothing to correct.)

Remember that you can click on any image or term anytime for more information. There's a built-in encyclopedia.

*(She heads over toward **JESSE**'s desk.)*

Hey Jesse.

(He doesn't hear her at first. She touches Jesse's shoulder. He hits pause on his tablet, takes out his headphones.)

JESSE. Hey.

SANDY. How's it going? Do you have any questions?

JESSE. Um, yeah, I did. But it told me to open up a chat window with a core teacher.

SANDY. Good. That's good. That's right.

Sorry if the videos are kind of – y'know. Lame.

JESSE. No they're actually, they're alright. They're kind of cool. I actually like wasted a bunch of time this weekend watching videos about like Oakland in the sixties and like, the Black Panthers and all that stuff. It's so crazy that it happened *right here* and I didn't know anything about it.

SANDY. Yeah, I wish we'd had time to talk about that in class, it's really complicated.

JESSE. It seems so cool. And it's cool to get to see everything. Instead of just trying to imagine it.

> (**SANDY** *doesn't say anything, just nods.* **JESSE** *puts on his headphones, gets back to his video.*)

SANDY. Any news from colleges?

> (*But* **JESSE** *can't hear her – he just stares at the screen.*)

> (*The brick wall rises behind the classroom, revealing row upon row of student desks, each with a glowing monitor on top of it, and* **SANDY** *is lost in a sea of them.*)

> (*She looks around, taking stock of her transformed classroom.*)

If anyone needs me...

> (*No answer.*)

> (*She strides to her desk. She packs up her stuff. She takes one last look at her classroom, and she walks out.*)

> (**JESSE** *looks at his computer. Then at where* **SANDY** *exited. He looks back and forth, uncertain of what to do.*)

> (**SANDY** *comes in and dumps her bag down.*)

WILL. How was your day.

SANDY. Um, you know – a little boring.

I thought the new features would be working by now.

WILL. Um, yeah, yeah, we built them. We've built most of them.

We're not sure exactly when we're going to roll them out.

SANDY. Well you know I could test them for you. Get the process started.

WILL. Are the kids getting bored?

SANDY. Not really. But. There's so much more we could do.

(**WILL** *sets his laptop down. He takes a second before he makes his next point.*)

WILL. Adam did a new round of customer interviews. It's been basically the only thing he's been doing. And you remember we commissioned that market study? We got the results back.

SANDY. Yeah?

WILL. Schools are looking for software that will let them trim their budgets.

They want to use it to support a higher ratio of students to teachers.

SANDY. Well that's stupid.

WILL. That's what they want.

SANDY. Well they want something stupid.

It's lucky for them they have smarter people like us designing it.

WILL. That's all they'll buy.

Almost every state has cut their education budget.

If the software's an added expense, schools can't afford it. If it saves them money...

SANDY. So you explain it to them. We pull together what parents have said, what psychologists have said –

WILL. Kids are having pretty good results on state tests with the software as it is. Better than in traditional classrooms.

SANDY. But state tests are ridiculous –

WILL. They're what counts.

SANDY. Um, not to me. Not to the *kids*.

WILL. But they're what *counts*.

SANDY. ...You already decided to do it.

WILL. No. We're still talking about it. We're trying to figure out if there's another way to push the advanced features. Or make different packages for different schools.

SANDY. You mean better packages for richer schools.

WILL. I don't have a choice Sandy.

SANDY. Well, you're the CEO, so you kind of do.

WILL. Someone's going to make this. If someone will pay for it, someone will make it. We have a lead right now, we have a slight lead, but we don't have dominance or anything. If we're not making what customers want they'll switch.

SANDY. You said more personal attention. That's what we talked about.

We said the kids who need it most would get more personal attention.

WILL. I still plan to do that.

SANDY. You're doing literally the opposite of that.

WILL. I still want to do that but you know what will mean that I definitely *can't* do that? You know what will mean that I *definitely* can't help kids is if my education startup fails, and I go back to making stupid dog apps, then I definitely can't help anybody.

SANDY. So you're saying that after you get all the teachers fired, you'll be in a great position to get them hired again? That's the argument?

WILL. This is how it works to run a company.

Everything you have, your clothes, your books, that bag, that mug, every single thing in this shitty apartment, you have because somebody made a million decisions that were difficult, and complicated, and gross.

I mean you say you want to run a school but do you know what it takes to run a school? Pleasing people, firing people, staying on budget, falling short of what you want to do. This is how the world works, this is real life.

SANDY. Please, tell me about reality Will, I know nothing about it. I have a different opinion from you, which means I must be wrong, please explain to me how ignorant I am.

WILL. I'm not saying that –

SANDY. I live in the real world Will, I live in a tough, tiring world, and you know how I deal with it? I work extra hard, I do the right thing and I try to convince other people to do the right thing. And it's hard work, but it's doable, and if everyone did it –

WILL. How did you get a promotion?

Was it acting like your usual self? Was it saying you wanted to undertake a long, slow, painful, expensive reform process, did that work well for you? Is that what did it?

(Beat.)

SANDY. You want to know what I think?

WILL. I know what you think.

SANDY.	**WILL.**
It's not like you make one compromise and then it will be smooth sailing. There will be more places where someone is telling you to do something you don't believe in and that is why you have to know what you won't do! You have to have guts.	I know that. I don't want to hear it. Don't try to teach me, I'm not a *student*!!

WILL. If I don't do this. And then some other company does it. And they're a success. I would never be okay. I would never be okay ever again.

SANDY. I don't run a successful company.

Am I some kind of loser?

Should I never be okay?

WILL. No. Of course not.

But I think you picked a job that pays shit.

I think you picked a job where we're never going to buy a house. We're never going to be able to send kids to college.

I think you picked a job where other people with more power than you make decisions.

And you hate that, you complain about that, but you don't have the power to change it.

You didn't get yourself in position to change anything.
Sandy. Someone is going to do this –

SANDY. Not necessarily.

WILL. Someone is. And if it's going to happen, we might as
well be the people in control.

SANDY. If I'm going to get screwed by a company I'd rather
you not be in charge of the company that does it.

WILL. That's illogical!

SANDY. People aren't *math*, Will.

WILL. We haven't decided on anything.
I want to know what you think.

SANDY. If I said don't do it, what would you say?

> *(Silence. A silence that becomes a little too
> long.)*

You know what Will? I think you should do whatever's
going to make you happy.

> *(She leaves.)*
>
> *(Music begins to play from offstage. Something
> celebratory and obnoxious.*)*
>
> *(It's six months later. An empty space in front
> of a brick wall.)*
>
> *(**WILL**'s alone with a red solo cup. He's drunk.)*
>
> *(**KAREN** enters.)*

WILL. Please don't tell me you came out here to check on
me.

KAREN. I came out here to get away from the dancing. It
was blinding me.
With science.
And incompetence.
They have Matty up in a chair as if it's his Bar Mitzvah.

---

*A license to produce *Start Down* does not include a performance
license for any third-party or copyrighted music. Licensees should create
an original composition or use music in the public domain. For further
information, please see Music Use Note on page 3.

WILL. Am I allowed to ask questions about her?

KAREN. Are you sure that's what you want to have on your mind right now?

You'll get to see her at the wedding.

WILL. How did you do it?

KAREN. Do what?

WILL. Forgive him.

KAREN. Well.

It was math.

I'm thirty-one. Sure I could have broken up with him in protest, but, math. Thirty-one. A year to fully get over it, two years to meet someone else, two more years to get engaged, a year to plan the wedding: Thirty-seven. I'd be lucky to get one kid out by that time. And I've always wanted three kids. And I want them with him.

But unfortunately for you, Sandy isn't good at math.

WILL. She's actually – she's pretty surprisingly good at it. She just doesn't like it that much.

KAREN. That comes out the same for your purposes.

WILL. Have they found her replacement yet?

KAREN. They made Welker the new department head. But they're not hiring a new teacher. The new target student-to-teacher ratio is fifty-to-one.

Sandy's in New York. She's living with her parents. Doing volunteer work.

She says she might want to run for Congress. "Take on the big problems."

> (**MATTY** *stumbles in, carrying a bong. He dances and hums along to the music, then stops dancing to take a hit.*)

MATTY. You want some?

WILL. No thanks.

MATTY. You're allowed to man.

You can calm down.

We did it.

(**ADAM** *enters. He approaches* **KAREN**, *kisses her.*)

ADAM. There you are.

The troops are calling for speeches.

And I think Will that that task falls first and foremost on you.

WILL. I'm not really a talker.

MATTY. Yeah man. Don't talk. Make.

(*He taps his bong against* **WILL***'s solo cup.*)

WILL. Don't do that.

MATTY. A little weed might do the trick man. Actually no you know what, coke is better for making speeches. I don't have any but I'm sure like twenty people at this party do.

KAREN. Don't tell me that.

MATTY. It's medicinal.

WILL. I don't know what to say.

KAREN. Say you're making something people love.

ADAM. Energizing the American economy.

MATTY. Making shit out of thin air.

ADAM. Say we're going to crush the competition.

MATTY. We're only going to get cooler.

KAREN. And we're going to work hard to reach the kids who need help the most.

ADAM. Yeah I'm not sure he's allowed to use that many clichés in one speech unless he's writing a football movie. But you'll be amazing.

And Karen can talk after about keeping innovation teacher-friendly.

KAREN. Absolutely.

WILL. Okay. You guys ready?

(**MATTY** *nods, takes one more hit, and goes.* **ADAM** *leads* **KAREN** *away.* **WILL** *follows them out. The music stops. Cheers and whoops and applause can be heard.*)

*(And then – total silence. **JESSE** comes out onto the stage alone. He faces upstage.)*

(The whole upstage wall begins to glow. It's a screen, with an image fading up.)

(It's like a video game. It shows the point of view of someone running through a forest. Branches get in the way; the runner almost trips. It's exciting.)

(Then we come up on a vista – a walled city.)

*(**E-KAREN**'s disembodied voice sounds from speakers all around the audience.)*

E-KAREN. *(Voice-over.)* Thank god you're back – your city needs your help. Which project do you want to tackle first?

*(Pop-up bubbles appear, offering **JESSE** options: "Advise the Government." "Build a Catapult." "Edit the General's Speech.")*

*(**JESSE** reaches up, as if he's using a huge touchscreen, and clicks "Build a Catapult.")*

*(A checklist of skills appears, a check next to "Angles," "Vectors," and "Weights." **JESSE** clicks on the only unchecked box – "Types of Wood.")*

(Two bubbles appear: "Read an Article," "Watch a Video [Recommended for You].")

*(**JESSE** reaches up, selects "Watch a Video." Three new bubbles appear: "Video from Alice." "Video from John." "Video from Carla.")*

(He clicks on "Video from John." A black male teacher with a set of props comes on.)

(A new bubble: "David's just started working on the same problem: Team up?")

(As the video continues, it gets faster and faster. Bubbles cover the video from John: "Prove You're Ready: Match Wits With a Botanist!" "More Review.")

(A game appears, matching botanical images to properties. The checklist reappears – "Types of Wood" is checked off.)

(More bubbles: "Find a Forest," "Study the Map," "Learn About Rainfall Patterns." "Recruit a Lumberjack," "Il Parle Francais!" "Which Way Will the Tree Fall?" "Message From the Governor!" "Give Him Three Examples From History," "Team up With Lisa," "Get the Materials Back to Camp," "Learn About Transportation.")

*(**JESSE** clicks and clicks and clicks, his movements becoming big, almost balletic.)*

(Then the screen goes black.)

*(**WILL**'s voice booms out, disembodied, from high above.)*

WILL. *(Voice-over.)* Gentlemen and gentlemen. Thank you for coming.

(The lights cut out.)

End of Play